Sleeping P

of glass

e's foot

bat for taste

rott apple core

goldenrod root

There's a little-known secret about Hildie Bitterpickles. She needs her sleep.

Every night Hildie brushes her teeth, puts away her spell book, and goes to bed with her cat, Clawdia.

Until the night when Hildie's quiet neighborhood changed.

Someone moved in next door. A very big someone. A very loud someone.

He was a giant. His house was two miles high with an elevator. But not just any kind of elevator. A beanstalk elevator. A noisy beanstalk elevator. It went **CLANGITY, CLANK, CLUNK** all night long.

"I can't sleep with
this racket!" cried Hildie.
She flew next door
and pulled the elevator plug
right out of the wall.
"That's better."

But the next day, there it was again. CLANGITY, CLANK, CLUNK. Even worse, someone had parked a gigantic shoe on the other side of Hildie's house.

"Howdy neighbor!" hollered an Old Lady.
Standing behind her were a GAZILLION
children. And guess what these children did?

"MY HOUSE!"
shouted Hildie.

Hildie was getting grouchier and grouchier when a Wolf showed up near a new brick house.

"Little Pig, little Pig, please let me in," he called.

"Not by the hairs of my chinny chin chin!" yelled the Pig.

So the Wolf huffed. . . and he puffed. . . and he accidentally blew the roof right off of the wrong house!

"Oops! Sorry!" said the Wolf.

"That's it!" Hildie stomped. "I'm moving!"

Hildie grabbed *The Daily Witch*.

THE DA

FIDDLERS WANTED!

Desperately seeking three fiddlers to round out King Cole's Court.

Must provide your own fiddle!

PAIL MISSING!

Help find my missing pail!

Last seen up the hill while I was fetching water.

REWARD AVAILABLE!

—Jack

CUPBOARD FOR SALE

Old Mother Hubbard's Antique Extravaganza

One slightly used cupboard for sale!

She began searching for a new home.

LY WITCH

REAL ESTATE CLASSIFIEDS

Are your neighbors driving you crazy?

Was the roof of your house recently blown off?

onty, the rat, can find you the home of your dreams or nightmares.

Stop by or call 1-888-RAT-REALTY.

Over 3 weeks of experience.

Specialty: Witch properties.

Customer satisfaction never guaranteed.

PEA-PROOF MATTRESSES!

Princess Mattresses are truly fit for royalty!

Don't lose another second of sleep to pesky peas

placed precisely under your posterior!

"I need a quiet house," said Hildie. "WITHOUT NEIGHBORS!"

"You've come to the right rat!" said Monty. He scampered through his files.

"This farmhouse with three blind mice seems promising."

"Are they *quiet* mice?" asked Hildie.

"Quiet as church mice!"

Hildie and Clawdia moved in.

That night, Hildie brushed her teeth, put away her spell book, and tucked Clawdia into bed. But as soon as the lights were out, guess who weren't so quiet after all?

All night long the blind mice scurried. But they didn't just scurry. They tinkered, hammered, and sawed. Because these weren't your ordinary blind mice. These were tinkering repair mice. Everywhere they went, it was

BANGITY BANG BRUM-BRUM!

"QUIET!" Hildie screamed.
She put in earplugs, buried her
head in pillows, and counted bats.
Nothing worked.

The next morning, Hildie called Monty. "It's me or the mice."
Monty searched his files. "How does a cottage sound? It even
comes with twenty black sheep."
"Are they *quiet* sheep?"
"Naturally!"

That day, Hildie and Clawdia
moved in.

That night, Hildie brushed her teeth, put away her spell book, and tucked Clawdia into bed. And guess who showed up when Hildie shut off the lamp?

"Excuse me," whispered a sheep, "Would you mind moving over?"

Then another crawled into bed. And another. And another.

Twenty BAA, BAA black sheep crawled into bed. Do you know how loud twenty snoring BAA, BAA black sheep can be?

The next morning, Hildie marched
herself to Monty's. "I'm done with sheep!"
Monty skimmed his files.
There was one house left.

RENTED

When they arrived, the house seemed noisy. . .
and roofless. . . and strangely familiar.

"Wait one eye-of-newt minute! This is *MY* house,"
said Hildie. "And my home! Come on, Clawdia. It's time
we talked to the neighbors."

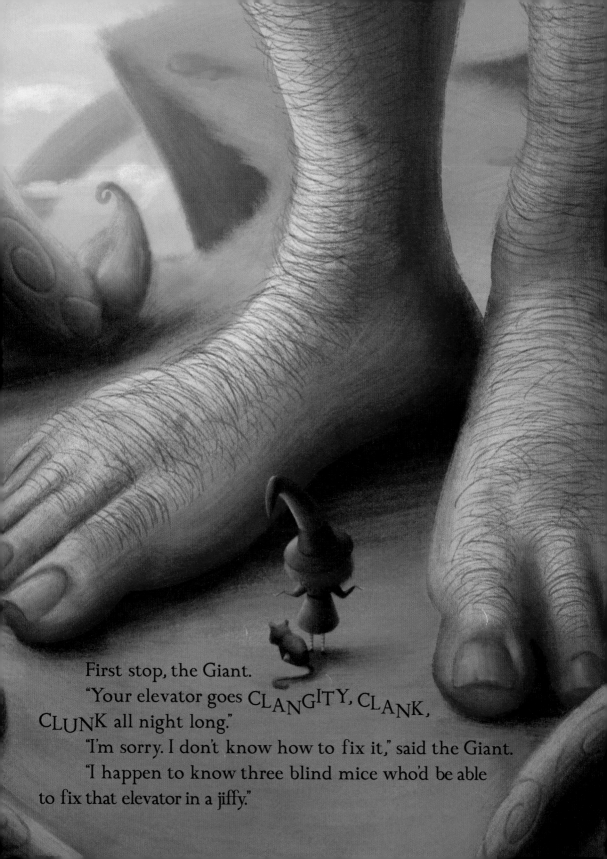

First stop, the Giant.

"Your elevator goes CLANGITY, CLANK, CLUNK all night long."

"I'm sorry. I don't know how to fix it," said the Giant.

"I happen to know three blind mice who'd be able to fix that elevator in a jiffy."

Next stop, the Old Lady.

"Your children have been playing baseball
all hours of the night!"

"Oh dear!" said the Old Lady, "The children
can't sleep in our new shoe. It's too quiet."

"Hmm...," said Hildie,
"I have an idea."

Finally, Hildie found the Wolf.

"Do you know anything about roof repair?" asked Hildie, "I could use a handy wolf around the house."

"My specialty is demolition, but I could give repair work a try."

That night, Hildie brushed her teeth, put away her
spell book, and tucked Clawdia into bed.

"Goodnight, Clawdia. Goodnight, neighbors," said Hildie.

And when Hildie turned out the lights, guess what she heard?

Nothing!

Robin Newman was a practicing attorney and legal editor, but she now prefers to write about witches, mice, pigs, and peacocks. Her previous book with Creston, *A Wilcox and Griswold Mystery: The Case of the Missing Carrot Cake* earned a starred review from Kirkus. She lives in New York, among many noisy neighbors.

Chris Ewald studied art at the Virginia Commonwealth University in Richmond. He works on art for videogames and animation. *Hildie Bitterpickles Needs Her Sleep* is his first picture book. He lives in Chesapeake, Virginia.

I've been spellbound by your magic since the day you were born.
For Noah, with all my love.
— R.N.

For my biggest fan, Bridget. I love you.
And for Marissa and Simon, thank you for your patience and grace.
— C.E.

Text copyright © 2016 Robin Newman
Illustartions copyright © 2016 Chris Ewald
Book design by Simon Stahl

Published by Creston Books, LLC
www.crestonbooks.co

Illustrations created using digital media.
Type set in Chanticleer, Wizard's Magic by Spideraysfonts, and Palooka by Blambot.

Source of Production:
Worzalla Books, Stevens Point, Wisconsin
Printed and bound in the USA

1 2 3 4 5

Creston Books